Lucky O'Leprechaun
COMES TO AMERICA

Lucky O'Leprechaun
COMES TO AMERICA

Written and Illustrated by Jana Dillon

PELICAN PUBLISHING COMPANY
Gretna 2002

First printing, September 2000
Second printing, September 2002

To my grandparents,
Richard Byrne from Ballard in Wicklow,
and Delia Dillon from Clough Mor in Galway

The word "Pelican" and the depiction of a pelican are trademarks
of Pelican Publishing Company, Inc., and are registered
in the U.S. Patent and Trademark Office.

Library of Congress Cataloging-in-Publication Data

Dillon, Jana
    Lucky O'Leprechaun comes to America / written and illustrated by Jana Dillon.
        p. cm.
    Sequal to: Lucky O'Leprechaun.
    Summary: When Great-uncle Patrick tries to give his grandnieces a treasure to take with them to America, he accidentally lures a leprechaun into their suitcases—with very lucky results.
    ISBN 1-56554-816-7 (alk. paper)
    [1. Irish Americans—Fiction. 2. Great-uncles—Fiction. 3. Leprechauns—Fiction.] I. Title.

    PZ7.D5795 Lug 2001
    [E]—dc21
                                                                00-039151

Printed in Korea

Published by Pelican Publishing Company, Inc.
1000 Burmaster Street, Gretna, Louisiana 70053

LUCKY O'LEPRECHAUN COMES TO AMERICA

Leprechauns like it just fine in Ireland, the land where they were born. So, how did the leprechauns in America get here? Most of them arrived the same way as that rogue Lucky O'Leprechaun.

Lucky lived close to the O'Brien cottage. Now old Uncle Patrick O'Brien had been taking care of his three wee grandnieces while their parents, Mr. and Mrs. O'Sullivan, were in America looking for the big house and the big job. He'd been busy all spring and summer with Kathleen, the daydreamer, Bridget, so sweet and gentle, and bossy Baby Moira.

But today Uncle Patrick was saying goodbye to the girls. "When you leave tomorrow morning to join your ma and da in America, I'll miss you so much," he said, with tears in his eyes. "I'll have no family here! I'll be all alone. Just myself alone."

"Come with us, Uncle Patrick!" begged sweet Bridget. "Come to America!"

"I wish I could," Uncle Patrick sighed, "but I'm too poor to afford the ticket."

"What are you talking about?" asked Kathleen, who hadn't been paying attention.

"Oh, pweez come," said Baby Moira. "Pweez, Uncle Paddy?" He shook his head no, so she stamped her foot. "Baby Moira say, 'Pweez!'"

"Alas, all I have in this world is the cow." He sighed, but his eyes twinkled. "And the treasure."

"The *treasure*?" repeated Bridget, as Kathleen snapped to attention.

"Hush!" said Uncle Patrick. "Come inside!" He tiptoed over to the windows and drew the curtains. "I've been saving the treasure all these years for you. 'Tis yours to take to America."

He reached up into the chimney and brought down an ancient box.

"I dug it up while plowing the field," said Patrick. "These old letters carved into the box spell *Brian Boru,* high king of Ireland in days gone by."

"'Tis one thousand years old!" whispered Kathleen. "Ooo, open it!"

Uncle Patrick passed out the
treasure. "Here, the crown, the
torque, and the gold of King Brian himself."

"Pretty!" cried Baby Moira.

Uncle Patrick clapped his hands in delight. "And you, being
O'Briens on your mother's side, are descended from Brian Boru.
It's only fitting that his treasure has come to you."

"No," said Kathleen, "we can't take it. You're poor. *You* need it."

"She's right," said Bridget, "Our da has a good job now in America."

"Then Baby Moira will take it," said Uncle Patrick. "Here, Moira."

"No!" shouted Baby Moira. She crossed her arms and frowned at him.

"You're a pack of stubborn donkeys!" cried Uncle Patrick. "You'll take it if I say so!"

"We love you, Uncle," said Bridget tenderly, "that's why we do this."

"We love you too much to take it," said Kathleen, hugging him.

"Love you, Uncle Paddy," said Baby Moira. She kissed his knee.

"Sure'n it looks like I'm defeated," said Uncle Patrick under their hugs. "Who can argue with the three of you?"

Later that evening didn't Uncle Patrick—the rogue!—send them outside to say goodbye to the cow. Then he sneaked into their room to their suitcases. He hid the torque in Kathleen's, the crown in Bridget's, and the bag of gold in Moira's.

"You can come in now, ladies," he called. "Kiss the cow goodbye. 'Tis tea time."

Not far from the cottage, Lucky O'Leprechaun was busy cobbling shoes. Suddenly he smelled the one thing he loved more than anything else in the world: *gold.*

"Now, surely that fine scent can't be coming from poor old Patrick O'Brien's cottage?" The leprechaun followed his nose to the open window.

"That's why my name is Lucky." He laughed. "'Tis gold, all right!"

With that, he leaped through the window and into Kathleen's suitcase. He surfaced with the torque. Then he burrowed down into Bridget's suitcase. "I remember this crown on the head of Brian Boru himself, how-are-ya! But I smell more gold!" He dived into Baby Moira's suitcase. "Brian's bag of gold! Hee hee!"

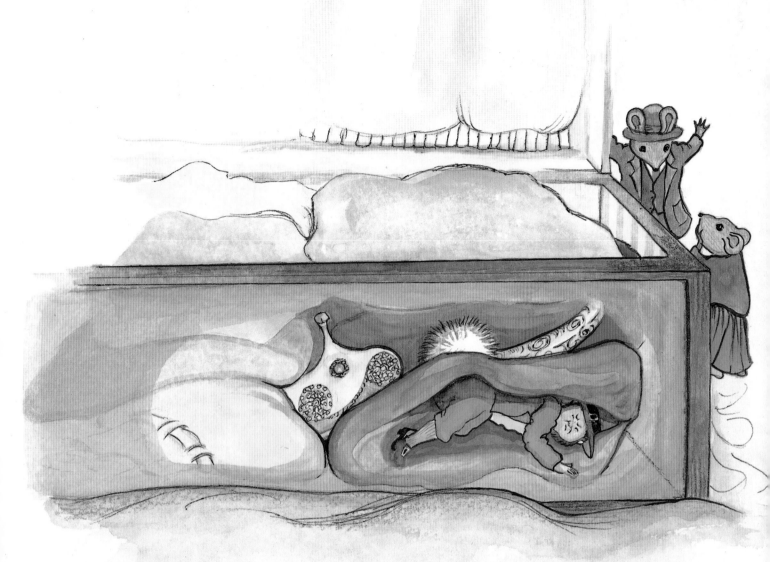

Just then, in walked the sisters with their rag dolls to pack.

"Begosh 'n' begorrah!" muttered Lucky, ducking. He pulled the treasures to the bottom of Baby Moira's suitcase and hid himself in her hat.

"Mine lumpy," said Baby Moira, pointing.

"There's something hard in Moira's suitcase," said Bridget.

Bridget fished around. Out came the treasure. "That Uncle Patrick!"

"How absent-minded of him," said Kathleen. "We told him 'tis his!"

"No, no, Kathleen," said Bridget. "He *hid* it for us. But he's the one who needs it. I'll hide it under our pillows. He'll find it after we're gone."

Bridget giggled and hid the gold, while Kathleen locked the suitcases.

Little did she know that she was locking Lucky O'Leprechaun inside.

The next morning Uncle Patrick said goodbye with tears pouring down his cheeks. "I'll never see you again. Never see you grow up! Never, never!"

"Of course you will," said Kathleen, "One gold coin buys a ticket."

Uncle Patrick smiled a bit, thinking the treasure was still hidden in their suitcases. "I would never touch it anyway. Not a cent. 'Tis yours."

The girls began to cry. "Then we truly *will* never see you again!"

On the boat to America, Lucky O'Leprechaun tried to escape every time Kathleen forgot to close Moira's suitcase, but Bridget was always too close and quick to lock it up.

To Lucky, locked inside the suitcase, the voyage seemed to take forever.

At last he felt the ship dock. He heard Mr. and Mrs. O'Sullivan smothering the girls with hugs and kisses. He heard them say they were driving in a car. "'Tis better than rocking on waves aboard ship," he muttered as he fell asleep.

Bam! Lucky was awakened when the suitcase was slammed onto the bed.

Kathleen opened Baby Moira's suitcase for her. The clothes shifted and out staggered the little manny in green, his head reeling.

"'Tis starving I am!" he muttered.

"Uncle packed us our own dear little pet leprechaun!" cried Kathleen.

"Pet?" Lucky O'Leprechaun looked up. "Musha!" he cried. He knew he couldn't escape with all three girls staring at him. People catch leprechauns by holding them in their sight. Unless all three children blinked at the same time, he was trapped. Of course, he could be set free if he granted them each a wish. But, wouldn't you know, leprechauns hate granting wishes—they're afraid someone might ask for their pot of gold.

He tried to trick them. "Have some manners! Close your eyes!"
But the three surprised sisters didn't even blink.
He tried to trick them again by sneezing loudly, "Archoo!"
Baby Moira blinked, but Kathleen and Bridget kept gazing at him.
"You creatures!" grumbled Himself, giving up. "Don't you kids know anything? If I grant you a wish, then I can go."

Sweet Bridget sighed. "I wish you were friendly."

"Granted, Bridget, me darling," said Himself with a bow. "For you, I'll be charming." He danced an Irish jig that set them all laughing.

"Now, Bridget, me honey darling," he said sweetly, "tell your sisters to *darken* my day with their *greedy* wishes."

"I have wish!" cried Baby Moira.

"No! Moira, don't. Wait for my help!" warned Kathleen. "Watch me, Moira. I wish," she said, "Uncle Patrick could live with us in America."

Suddenly, downstairs they heard their mother shout, "Patrick!" and their father boom, "Welcome!" and Uncle Patrick say, "'Tis the strangest thing . . . I just blinked and I was here!"

Lucky O'Leprechaun whispered to Baby Moira, "Quick! What's your wish?"

Kathleen didn't notice his trick. She was daydreaming about wishes.

"Wait, Moira!" warned Bridget. "Kathleen, she'll wish for candy or a doll!"

But stubborn Baby Moira wouldn't wait.

"I wish treasures!" cried Baby Moira. "I want torque, crown, bag of gold!"

Suddenly Baby Moira was wearing the crown and the torque, and holding the bag of gold.

For a brief moment, Lucky O'Leprechaun stared at his beloved, the gold, then he said, "Ta ta, Bridget, me darling," and leaped out the window into their garden.

Kathleen and Bridget cried, "Good job, Moira!" and they clapped their hands.

"These are O'Brien family heirlooms," said Kathleen.

"Let's keep them in the family forever," said Bridget, "for their history."

"Pretty," said Baby Moira. "Pretty treasure."

"And their beauty," said Bridget.

Then the three sisters raced downstairs to show the family the treasures and to wish Uncle Patrick *cead mille failte*—a hundred thousand welcomes to America.

Out in the garden Lucky O'Leprechaun set up his house, fine as you please, under a thornbush. Then he went out to explore his new American neighborhood, with his nose at the ready to sniff out his great love, gold.